Let's Eat Together

Reid Kaplan

This book is dedicated to my smart, beautiful daughter Charlie, who will always be my best creation. I love you to the moon and back infinity times. Remember to always reach for the moon. You can do whatever you put your brilliant, kind, and creative mind to.

I love you Charlie.

Written by: Reid Kaplan
Edited by: Amanda "Roomie" Robinson
Illustrated by: Ambadi Kumar

www.letseattogetherbook.com

Made in USA

ISBN: 978-0-692-14679-8

Come one, come all,

Let's join together and have a ball.

Are you hungry? So are we.
Don't be shy, sit down and eat.

Mrs. Cat, Mr. Dog

Señor Bird, Monsieur Frog.

There's a wolf, there's a lamb
A spotted rabbit we all call Sam.

A dragonfly, a porcupine
a grizzly bear with his clementine.

A mama pig, a daddy goat
A baby cow with a
black and white coat.

A hedgehog, a butterfly
A giant turtle eating pie!

A grandma duck, a grandpa goose
sitting across from a spider
and a moose.

A pelican, a silly snake
All on a bench, next to the lake.

Pass the broccoli, pass the melon

Fresh berries, and veggies,

Mr. Deer is in heaven!

All are invited to join in on the feast

Bring your good manners and

don't be a beast.

We all might look different, and
think different too.
If we can all get along then so
can all of you.

Written by Reid Kaplan
Edited by Amanda "Roomie" Robinson
illustrations by Ambadi Kumar
copyright ©2018

Made in USA